This book belongs to

....

Walt Disney's
Donald Duck's Toy Sailboat

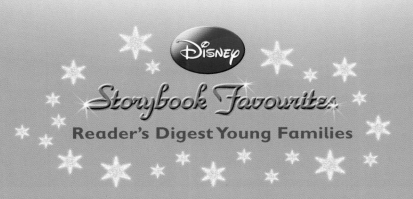

Disney

Storybook Favourites

Reader's Digest Young Families

Illustrations by The Walt Disney Studios

Story by Annie North Bedford

Illustrations adapted by Samuel Armstrong
from the motion picture *Chips Ahoy*

Walt Disney's
Donald Duck's Toy Sailboat

'There!' said Donald Duck. 'At last it's done!'

He stood back to look at his toy sailboat. Making it had been a big job. It had taken him all summer long. But now the boat was finished. And it was a beautiful boat.

The mantelpiece was just the place for it, too. The whole room looked better with the sailboat up there.

'Building sailboats is hungry work,' Donald said to himself. So he made himself a great big lunch.

'Now to try out the boat in the lake,' he thought. But his hard work had made him sleepy, too. So Donald settled down for a nap after lunch. After that he would try out the boat.

Now outside Donald's cottage, in the old elm tree, lived two little chipmunks, Chip and Dale. And they had had no lunch at all.

'I'm hungry,' said Chip, rubbing his empty tummy.

'Me too,' said little Dale. But suddenly he brightened. 'Look!' he said.

Chip looked and looked. At last he spied it – one lone acorn still clinging to the bough of an oak down beside the lake.

Down the elm tree they raced, across to the oak and up its rough-barked trunk.

'Mine!' cried Chip, reaching for the nut.

'I saw it first!' Dale cried.

So they pushed and they tugged and they tussled, until the acorn slipped through their fingers and fell *kerplunk* into the lake.

The two little chipmunks looked very sad as they watched the acorn float away. But Dale soon brightened. 'Look!' he cried.
Chip looked. On a little island out in the middle of the lake stood a great big oak tree weighed down with acorns on every side.

Down to the shore the chipmunks ran. But *br-r-r!* It was too cold to swim.

'How can we get to them?' wondered Chip.

'I don't know,' said Dale. But he soon had an idea. 'Look in there!' he said.

On the mantelpiece in Donald Duck's cottage they could see the toy sailboat.

'Come on,' said Dale. So away they raced, straight up to the door and into the cottage.

They had the sailboat down and almost out the door when Donald stirred in his sleep.

'Nice day for a sail,' he said dreamily, as the boat slipped smoothly past his eyes.

Soon afterwards, Donald woke up completely.
'Now to try out my boat,' he cried.
Suddenly something outside the window caught his eye. It was his sailboat, out on the lake!

'I'll fix those chipmunks!' Donald said.

He pulled out his fishing rod and reel, and chose a painted float that looked just like a nut.

'This will do,' Donald grinned.

From the pier he cast − as far as he could fling that little
float and hook. With a *plop* it landed beside the toy boat.

'Look! Look at this!' cried Dale. He leaned right over the edge of the boat to pull in the float.

'Great! A nut!' said Chip. 'We'll toss it in the hold and have it for supper tonight.'

As soon as the nut was fast in the hold, Donald pulled in the line. He pulled that little boat right in to shore. The chipmunks never suspected a thing. They did not even notice Donald pouring water into the cabin of the boat.

Chip discovered that when he went into the cabin. 'Man the pumps!' he cried.

Those two chipmunks worked with might and main while Donald watched and laughed.

'Ha ha!' At Donald's chuckle, the chipmunks looked up.
'So that's the trouble!' Dale cried.
He pulled the acorn float up out of the hold and flung it at
Donald so that he was soon tangled up in fishing line.

While Donald tried to pull himself free, the chipmunks set sail once more.

Before Donald could launch his swift canoe, they had reached the island's shore.

    As Donald was paddling swiftly along, he heard a sharp
rat-a-tat-tat!
    The oak tree on the island seemed to shiver and shake as its
store of acorns rained down.

The busy little chipmunks finished dancing on the branches. Then they hauled their harvest on board.

'Oh, well,' said Donald, watching from his canoe. 'At least now I know the sailboat really will sail. Now let's just see what those little fellows do.'

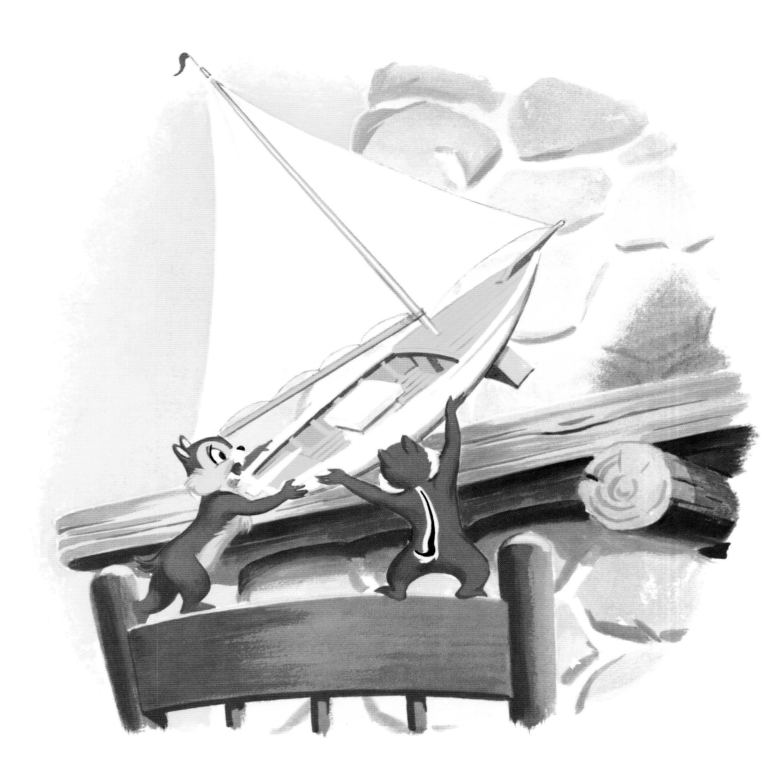

And can you guess what the chipmunks did? They stored their nuts in a hollow tree. And they took Donald's toy sailboat straight back, and put it on the mantelpiece where it belonged!

Walt Disney's Donald Duck's Toy Sailboat is a *Disney Storybook Favourites* book

Walt Disney's Donald Duck's Toy Sailboat, copyright © 1954, 2006 Disney Enterprises, Inc.
Story by Annie North Bedford. Illustrations adapted by Samuel Armstrong from the motion picture *Chips Ahoy.*

This edition was adapted and published in 2009 by
The Reader's Digest Association Limited
11 Westferry Circus, Canary Wharf, London E14 4HE

Editor: Rachel Warren Chadd
Designer: Louise Turpin
Design consultant: Simon Webb

® Reader's Digest, the Pegasus logo and Reader's Digest Young Families
are registered trademarks of
The Reader's Digest Association, Inc.

We are committed both to the quality of our products
and the service we provide to our customers.
We value your comments, so please do contact us on
08705 113366 or via our website at
www.readersdigest.co.uk
If you have any comments or suggestions
about the content of our books, email us at
gbeditorial@readersdigest.co.uk

Printed in China

A Disney Enterprises/Reader's Digest Young Families Book

ISBN 978 0 276 44474 6
Book code 641-033 UP0000-1
Oracle code 504400087H.00.24